MEET ALL THESE FRIENDS IN BUZZ BOOKS:

Thomas the Tank Engine
The Animals of Farthing Wood
Biker Mice From Mars
James Bond Junior
Fireman Sam
Joshua Jones
Rupert
Babar

First published in Great Britain 1993 by Buzz Books,
an imprint of Reed Children's Books
Michelin House, 81 Fulham Road, London, SW3 6RB
and Auckland, Melbourne, Singapore and Toronto
Reprinted 1994

ISBN 1 85591 328 3

Printed in Italy by Olivotto

Journey's
End

Story by Colin Dann
Text by Mary Risk
Illustrations by The County Studio

White Deer Park was finally in reach.
From the crest of the hill Fox could see the
beautiful waving treetops of the nature
reserve. But the animals of Farthing Wood
were scattered far and wide. They'd had a
great fright, and had run off in all different
directions. Fox would have to gather all
the animals, and lead them to the safety of
White Deer Park together.

"We'll have to find the others," he said.

"Why?" asked Hare. "They'll find their way to the park on their own. Let's go now."

Mole looked worried. "We can't go without Badger," he said. "We won't leave Badger behind, will we, Fox?"

"Well, Fox?" called Owl from above. "You got us into this mess. How are you going to get us out of it?"

Badger and Weasel were hiding in town. They had slipped through a trap door and into a cool, dark storage cellar.

"This is fun!" said Weasel, dancing about on a stack of crates. "What an adventure!"

"Don't you care about the others?" growled Badger. "They might be in danger."

Weasel laughed. "Don't worry so much, Badger. I'm sure they're fine."

"I am worried, Weasel," said Badger seriously. "I think right now we should try to get some sleep. We'll need all our energy to search for Fox and Mole, and our other friends."

Weasel scampered down from the crates and slid across the floor. "Wheee! I'm having too much fun to sleep!"

On the edge of town, the squirrels were clinging to the top of a telephone pole, looking about for their friends.

"I can't see anyone," said one squirrel.

"Neither can I," said the other.

They didn't hear the squeaks of the voles, mice and shrews who were hiding in the long grass nearby.

There was a rustle in the grass, and Adder's forked tongue snapped out at the little animals.

"I thought I heard a sssqueak," she said.

The animals bolted with fear.

"What fun! Hide and ssseek!" hissed Adder, and she wriggled off after them.

Just outside the town, the rabbits had fallen into a deep ditch.

"I think I've broken my leg," wailed Father Rabbit.

"No, you haven't," replied Mother Rabbit. "You just like complaining."

"It's all right for you," grumbled Father Rabbit, "but I'm quite fragile." He hobbled about at the bottom of the ditch. "Oh dear, how are we going to get out of here?"

Back on the hilltop, Fox was thinking.

"This is a job for the birds," he said at
last. "Owl, Kestrel and Whistler, you must
go and find the other animals and bring
them back here."

"Ridiculous idea!" hooted Owl. "They'll
be in hiding. We'll never find them."

"But you're such a good hunter, Owl,"
said Fox. "Surely you'll be able to spot
our friends."

"Very well," said Owl, looking pleased.
The three birds flew off into the sky.

Weasel was sleepy.

"Weasel, keep awake, please," said Badger crossly.

"I'm trying," replied Weasel with a yawn.

From outside came a thud. Then another thud, and another. A trolley piled high with crates rolled down the ramp into the storage cellar. Badger and Weasel dodged out of the way just in time!

Then Weasel did a quick U-turn, and leapt up the ramp and out to the street.

Badger followed, but he wasn't as quick as Weasel, and narrowly missed colliding with another trolley as it rolled down the ramp and into the cellar.

The stores manager gazed after the animals in astonishment as they raced past her.

By the time they rounded the corner, Weasel was exhausted.

"I'm so sleepy, Badger," she said, closing her eyes. "You'll have to carry me!"

Kestrel flew high in the air, scanning the ground with her powerful eyes.

"Kee! The squirrels!" she called, and dived down to the telephone pole.

The squirrels slid to the ground, chattering with relief.

"Follow me! Kee! Kee!" called Kestrel.

16

Fox saw the squirrels coming.

"Thank goodness you're safe!" he said. "Is there any sign of the others?"

"No," the squirrels replied, shaking their heads.

Mole began to cry.

"It's all right, matey," croaked Toad. "I know Badger's safe. I can feel it in my bones!"

Suddenly, the animals heard a grunting
sound, and a weary Badger appeared.
Weasel was fast asleep on his back.

"We've found you at last!" exclaimed
Badger, looking round at his friends.

He stooped down, letting Weasel slide
to the ground, where she continued to
snore happily.

"Oh, Badger," said Mole, running to greet
his friend, "I'm so happy to see you!"

Badger put out a great paw, and lifted the
little animal into his arms.

The mice, voles and shrews had scurried away from Adder as quickly as they could. Now they came to a wide grassy slope.

"Is Adder still behind us?" asked a mouse.

Adder reared her head. "Yesss, I'm right here," she said. "Thisss game isss fun!"

The animals dashed into a sandy bunker.

As Father Vole peered out, a golf ball whizzed past his nose! Kestrel's keen eyes spotted him, and she swooped down.

"Follow me!" she called.

As the animals scrambled onto the green, Kestrel spied a huge mowing machine approaching rapidly!

"Come on," she called. "Hurry!"

"Yesss, hurry!" hissed Adder, sliding up behind the frightened animals.

They sprinted away from the mower just in time, but Adder was too late. With a flick of her tail, she escaped down a golf hole.

"Bravo, Adder!" cried Kestrel.

Whistler found the rabbits in the ditch.

"Please get us out!" said Father Rabbit.

"Hmm, this could be tricky," said Whistler.
He bent down and Mother Rabbit hopped
onto his back. Then she climbed up his long
neck, and then with one more mighty hop,
she was out of the ditch.

But Father Rabbit was too heavy.
Whistler's legs sagged under the weight,
and he couldn't stand up.

"I'll have to go for help," he said.

"You'll leave me here. I know you will!"
cried Father Rabbit.

"Don't worry, I'll be back soon," Whistler
replied calmly, as he flapped away.

He landed beside Fox.

"I've found the rabbits," he said. "Father Rabbit is stuck in a ditch."

"Well done, Whistler," said Fox. "I'll go and get them now."

"Do be careful, Fox," said Mole. "Rabbits can get into all kinds of trouble."

Fox found Father Rabbit sitting in a puddle at the bottom of the ditch.

"What took you so long?" grumbled Father Rabbit. "I've got a broken leg, you know."

Fox ran down into the ditch. "Hop onto my back," he told Father Rabbit.

With a skip and a jump, they were out of the ditch.

"Er, thank you, Fox," said Father Rabbit.

Then he and Mother Rabbit hopped away.

"My pleasure," replied Fox, shaking his head in amusement.

By now Adder had found the rest of the
animals. She leered greedily at a vole.

"I promisssed not to eat you during our
journey," she hissed. "But the journey isss
nearly over. I can't wait!"

Badger watched her slither away.

"Don't worry," he told the anxious voles.
"Adder may want to behave like other
snakes, but I can see the journey has
changed her. It's changed us all."

"I feel almost sad now the journey's over," said Father Vole.

"I'll be glad to arrive at White Deer Park," said Mother Vole. "But even then we'll never be ordinary voles again. We're the animals of Farthing Wood, and we shall keep the spirit of our journey for ever and ever."

"Well said, Mother Vole," said Fox. "And now, everyone, follow me. We are going to White Deer Park."

One by one, the animals entered the nature reserve. A huge stag was waiting to greet them.

"It's him, mateys!" gasped Toad. "The Great White Stag! We've made it at last!"

"Well done, my friends," the Stag said.
"News of your great journey reached us
long ago. Welcome to White Deer Park."

He turned, and the animals of Farthing Wood
trotted after him into their new home.